JUPITER'S LEGACY

VOLUME 1

MARK MILLAR
WRITER

WILFREDO TORRES
ARTIST (CHAPTER 1, 2, 3, 6)

DAVIDE GIANFELICE
Pencils & Inks
(CHAPTER 3-PAGES 8, 13, 14, 21, **4, 5**)

FRANCESCO MORTARINO
Inks
(CHAPTER 3-PAGES 8, 13, 14, 21, **4, 5**)

IVE SVORCINA
Colors

PETER DOHERTY
Letters & Design

FRANK QUITELY
Cover & Chapter Illustrations
(COLOR CHAPTER 5 by **NATHAN FAIRBAIRN**)

NICOLE BOOSE
Editor

PETER DOHERTY & DREW GILL
Production

MELINA MIKULIC
2020 Collection Cover Design

LUCY MILLAR
CEO

IMAGE COMICS, INC. · Robert Kirkman: Chief Operating Officer · Erik Larsen: Chief Financial Officer · Todd McFarlane: President · Marc Silvestri: Chief Executive Officer · Jim Valentino: Vice President · Eric Stephenson: Publisher / Chief Creative Officer · Jeff Boison: Director of Sales & Publishing Planning · Jeff Stang: Director of Direct Market Sales · Kat Salazar: Director of PR & Marketing · Drew Gill: Cover Editor · Heather Doornink: Production Director · Nicole Lapalme: Controller · IMAGECOMICS.COM

CHAPTER 1

"THIS IS THE RESTING PLACE OF THE WORLD'S GREATEST HEROES.

"THESE ARE THEIR ADVENTURES.

"THEIR POWERS BESTOWED BY A MYSTERIOUS ISLAND, SIX FRIENDS CAME TOGETHER TO FIGHT INJUSTICE.

"DEDICATED TO PEACE AND FREEDOM, THEIR ONLY DESIRE WAS TO HELP OTHER PEOPLE...

"...AND TO SERVE HUMANITY UNTIL THEIR FINAL BREATH."

1959:

IF YOU'RE HUNGRY I'D RECOMMEND THE BANANA SPLIT. IF YOU'RE NOT JUST GO WITH THE TULIP SUNDAE...

WHAT IN GOD'S NAME...?

HOW DO YOU KNOW *DANNY?*

WE USED TO BE IN THE *MARINES* TOGETHER. HE'S HOOKED ME UP WITH A FEW TRICKS BEFORE, BUT NONE OF THEM WERE AS HANDSOME AS YOU.

DID YOU KNOW HE HOOKS UP ALL THE *MOVIE STARS* AT THAT GAS STATION? I SAW *TYRONE POWER* OUT THERE AND WALTER PIDGEON GAVE ME TWENTY BUCKS JUST TO GIVE HIM A *HAND JOB.*

OH, YEAH?

SO WHAT LINE OF WORK ARE *YOU* IN?

NOBODY'S SURE EXACTLY HOW IT GOT HERE. CARRIED ON THE SPACE WINDS? I GUESS IT'S NOT IMPORTANT.

ALL THAT MATTERS IS THAT IT DUG DOWN DEEP AND STARTED TO FEED ON THE MEMORIES OF THE *LOCALS*.

THAT'S WHAT IT *ATE*, YOU SEE.

HUMAN MEMORY.

FITZ WAS DOWN... WALTER HAD BEEN SUBDUED...

I WAS STARTING TO BUCKLE TOO, DATES OF BIRTHDAYS ALREADY FADING, THE SMELL OF MY FATHER'S COLOGNE GONE FOREVER.

HOW COULD I FIGHT A PSYCHIC ASSAULT IF EVEN *WALTER'S* BRAIN HAD BEEN TAKEN OVER?

WHAT THE HELL?

TAKE IT EASY, RICHARD. I JUST BUILT SOMETHING TO CREATE A SONIC BOOM.

OUR WORLD'S CEPHALOPODS ARE SENSITIVE TO SOUND SO I DIDN'T SEE WHY THIS THING WOULD BE *DIFFERENT.*

UNION HQ:

I BELIEVE THIS CALLS FOR A LITTLE CELEBRATION...

...ALIEN SQUID RETURNED TO SPACE AND NO CIVILIAN CASUALTIES. IS THIS WHAT THEY CALL A *JOB WELL DONE?*

I STILL DON'T SEE WHY WE ALWAYS NEED A *SOUVENIR.* WE'RE GOING TO RUN OUT OF *SPACE* IN HERE.

SO I'LL BUY US A NEW BUILDING, HOT-STUFF. BESIDES, I *LIKE* TROPHIES. THEY REMIND ME HOW *WONDERFUL* I AM AT THINGS.

HAS ANYONE HAD A CHANCE TO LOOK AT THAT PROPOSAL FROM THE *FBI?* I WAS READING IT IN MY LUNCH BREAK AND THERE SEEMS TO BE SOME *GOOD IDEAS.*

TO BE HONEST, I'M UNCOMFORTABLE ABOUT AFFILIATING WITH *ANY* GOVERNMENT BODY, WALTER.

I RESPECT MISTER HOOVER'S RECORD AT THE BUREAU, BUT I'VE ALWAYS BELIEVED WE NEED TO *STAY ABOVE* POLITICS.

NOW WOULD ANYONE LIKE TO JOIN ME FOR *POST*-POST-BATTLE COCKTAILS AT THE WHISKEY LOUNGE? IT'S ONLY MIDNIGHT AND MY BREAKFAST WON'T BE READY FOR ANOTHER *TWELVE HOURS.*

I THINK THAT'S MY CUE TO TAKE OFF.

WHAT ABOUT YOU, FITZ? STILL PUTTING THOSE WIFE AND KIDS BEFORE YOUR *DRINKING COMPADRES?*

I AM *SO TIRED,* GEORGE. SERIOUSLY, THE BABY HAS US UP AT FOUR. I'LL GET THREE HOURS' SLEEP AS IT IS.

I'D TAG ALONG, BUT I'M AFRAID SOME OF US HAVE A HOT DATE BACK IN *LA.*

OH, REALLY? SOMETHING *DELICIOUS,* I HOPE?

ONE OF MY NURSES.

BLONDE. A MOUTH LIKE KIM NOVAK...

LOS ANGELES:

JESUS.

MOVE! IT'S THE COPS!

OH GOD! MY WIFE IS GONNA *KILL* ME!

MONDAY MORNING, AUGUST 4, 1959

ER THE LAW

FIVE ARRESTS IN L.A. ... RAID

IT COULD HAVE BEEN *ME*, DANNY...

SERIOUSLY, CAN YOU IMAGINE WHAT WOULD HAVE HAPPENED IF I'D GOT MYSELF *ARRESTED?*

WHAT ARE YOU DOING AT THE PARK *ANYWAY?* YOU KNOW THE COPS JUST SIT THERE WAITING.

YOU'VE GOT *ME* TO HOOK YOU UP IF YOU'RE LOOKING FOR A NEW TRICK. WHY WOULD YOU TAKE THE RISK?

GOLF

GOLF

GOLF

I KNOW, I KNOW. I JUST GET *RECKLESS* SOMETIMES. I WAS JUST FEELING COCKY AFTER BEATING THAT *SPACE MONSTER.*

CAN YOU IMAGINE WHAT THE *TEAM* WOULD HAVE SAID? ALL THE *GOOD THINGS* I'VE DONE... ALL THE *SUPERHERO STUFF...* IT WOULDN'T COUNT FOR *ANYTHING.*

MY FAMILY'S IN *POLITICS* BACK IN SAN FRANCISCO. DO YOU REALIZE WHAT THIS WOULD HAVE DONE TO THEIR *REPUTATION?*

I HAVE TO SAY I FIND THE WHOLE THING *RIDICULOUS*, RICHARD...

...SURE, HALF OF HOLLYWOOD'S IN LAVENDER MARRIAGES, BUT AT LEAST WE'RE *HANDSOMELY PAID* TO BE HYPOCRITES.

YOU'RE OUT THERE SAVING LIVES EVERY DAY. WHY SHOULD *YOU* HAVE TO LIE ABOUT WHO YOU'RE SNUGGLING UP WITH EVERY NIGHT?

IT'S LIKE POLITICIANS AND PREACHERS, KATIE. THE PUBLIC JUST HOLD US TO A HIGHER STANDARD. PEOPLE WANT THEIR SUPERHEROES TO BE *WHITER THAN WHITE.*

WELL, I'M JUST WORRIED WHAT IT DOES TO YOUR *HEALTH,* DARLING. I'VE SEEN WHAT LIVING A LIE CAN DO.

WE'RE A QUEER TOWN SELLING THE WORLD A HETEROSEXUAL IDEAL. HAVEN'T YOU EVER WONDERED WHY WE'RE ALL ON *PILLS AND BOOZE?*

A DOUBLE LIFE IS A TERRIBLE STRAIN AND YOU'RE LIVING A *TRIPLE LIFE.* THE STRESS MUST BE *UNBEARABLE.*

JESUS, KATIE. I CAME HERE TO GET *CHEERED UP.*

RICHARD, MEET FRANK WHO DOES MY GARDENS. FRANK, RICHARD IS A DEAR, DEAR FRIEND. WOULD YOU MIND CHEERING HIM UP?

TO TELL YOU THE TRUTH, I DON'T KNOW HOW *SOCIABLE* I'M FEELING RIGHT NOW.

KLICK

KLICK

KLICK

ST THOMAS' HOSPITAL:

DOCTOR CONRAD, I'M FEDERAL AGENT CLYDE TOLSON. DIRECTOR HOOVER ASKED ME TO LET YOU KNOW HE'S WAITING FOR YOU IN YOUR OFFICE.

WHAT?

WELL, *SOMEBODY'S* BEEN A NAUGHTY BOY.

I WONDER WHAT YOUR FRIENDS ON THE TEAM WOULD THINK IF THEY SAW ALL THE DISGUSTING THINGS YOU'VE BEEN GETTING UP TO IN YOUR SPARE TIME.

OH MY GOD.

OF COURSE, THIS DOESN'T HAVE TO BE A *COMPLETE* DISASTER...

CHAPTER 2

UTOPIAN! HAVE YOU LOST YOUR *MIND?*

MY DOOM-DROID HAS THE POWERS OF THIS WORLD'S GREATEST HEROES. YOU CAN'T HIDE FROM HIM BEHIND A *PAIR OF GLASSES.*

NO, BUT THEY'RE THE KEY TO HIS *DEFEAT.*

WHERE'S HE GOING?

STAND BACK! HE'S GOING TO NEED *SPACE!*

UNLIKE THE REST OF THE TEAM I'VE GOT THREE DIFFERENT IDENTITIES.

THE FIRST IS A SUPERHERO AND IDOL TO MILLIONS.

THE SECOND IS A NEONATAL SURGEON AT THE PRESBYTERIAN HOSPITAL.

THE THIRD IS A SECRET HOMOSEXUAL WHO ENDANGERS THE LIVES AND REPUTATIONS OF ALL THE PEOPLE *CLOSEST* TO HIM.

I'LL SAY IT AGAIN SO WE'RE ABSOLUTELY CLEAR, DOCTOR CONRAD...

...YOU EITHER GIVE ME THE NAMES OF ALL YOUR TEAMMATES OR EVERY NEWS AGENCY IN THIS COUNTRY IS GOING TO SEE THESE PICTURES.

CAN YOU IMAGINE WHAT THE *UTOPIAN* WOULD SAY? OR THAT VERY RESPECTABLE FAMILY OF YOURS UP IN SAN FRANCISCO?

HOOVER, *PLEASE*...

GIVE ME THEIR NAMES INSIDE FORTY-EIGHT HOURS...

...AND SPECIAL AGENT TOLSON AND I MAKE THIS ALL *GO AWAY.*

THE CRAZY THING IS THEY'VE BEEN GOING AT IT LIKE RABBITS.

WHO?

J EDGAR HOOVER AND THIS SPECIAL AGENT TOLSON GUY. THE STORY GOES THEY'VE BEEN LOVERS FOR YEARS, BUT IT DOESN'T STOP THEM BLACKMAILING *OTHER PEOPLE*.

THIS *DOESN'T HELP* ME, DANNY. I'M HARDLY GOING TO TAKE ON THE *FBI*.

YOU COULD ALWAYS DO WHAT THE *ACTORS* DO AND TIE THE KNOT WITH SOME POOR BROAD.

THERE'S A SCI-FI NOVELIST STARTED A CHURCH AND HE'S ALWAYS ON THE LOOKOUT FOR CELEBRITIES HE CAN HELP.

HE COULD FIX YOU UP WITH A WIFE *TONIGHT* AND ALL YOU NEED TO DO IS GO TO A FEW OF HIS *PUBLIC MEETINGS*.

GDIF TIRE SAL

DISCOUNT PRICE ON ALL GRADES & SIZE BIG INVENTOR

I CAN'T JUST *MARRY* SOMEONE. BESIDES, THEY'VE GOT *PHOTOS.*

SO MAYBE YOU JUST *COME CLEAN.*

TELL THE WORLD I'M *QUEER?* ARE YOU OUT OF YOUR *MIND?*

I'D LOSE MY *JOB.* I'D HAVE TO LEAVE *THE UNION.* MY FAMILY WOULD BE *DISGRACED.*

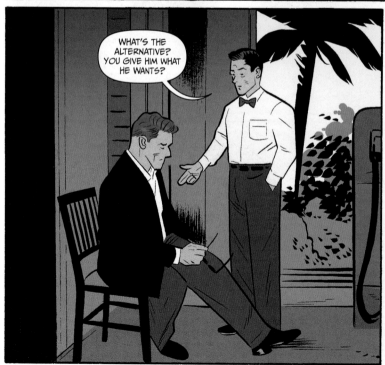

WHAT'S THE ALTERNATIVE? YOU GIVE HIM WHAT HE WANTS?

I *ENVY* HOW NORMAL THE REST OF YOU ARE.

SHELDON AND HIS LOVELY JANE. FITZ AND HIS BEAUTIFUL FAMILY...

...GEORGE DOING PUSH-UPS ON THE BAR, ALWAYS TRYING TO IMPRESS *THE GIRLS*.

WHY AM *I* THE ONE WHO HAD TO BE ABNORMAL?

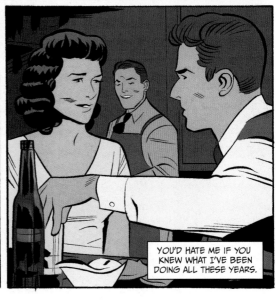

YOU'D HATE ME IF YOU KNEW WHAT I'VE BEEN DOING ALL THESE YEARS.

TWELVE MORE HOURS, DOCTOR CONRAD. I'M ABSOLUTELY SERIOUS.

I'D TELL HIM I DIDN'T CARE, BUT IT'S MORE THAN JUST *MY* REPUTATION.

WE WERE GIVEN THESE POWERS TO INSPIRE THE WORLD AND A SUPERHERO - MORE THAN ANYONE - MUST NEVER HAVE A *SCANDAL.*

JESUS CHRIST.

WHAT HAPPENED, GRACE?

HE SWALLOWED SOME PILLS AND CUT HIS WRISTS. HE'D HAVE BLED TO DEATH IF FITZ HADN'T WALKED IN AND FOUND HIM IN THE BATHTUB.

YOU DON'T THINK YOU'RE GETTING OUT OF THIS *THAT* EASILY, DO YOU?

OH NO.

GIVE ME THEIR *NAMES*, YOU LITTLE DRAMA QUEEN.

YOU NEED TO *TOUGHEN UP*, SON. BECAUSE THIS DOESN'T STOP HERE. I'VE GOT JOBS LINED UP AT HOME AND ABROAD TO KEEP YOU BUSY FOR A *LONG, LONG* TIME.

IT GOES WITHOUT SAYING I WANT INTEL ON THE SOVIETS, BUT THERE'S ENEMIES HERE I'D LIKE MONITORED TOO AND I'M NOT A MAN WHO LACKS AMBITION.

HELL, I BET YOU COULD TAKE ME TO THE *WHITE HOUSE* IF YOU REALLY PUT YOUR MIND TO IT.

NEVER.

EXCUSE ME?

THESE POWERS ARE FOR *THE WORLD*. NOT *YOU*.

WELL, THE WORLD IS ABOUT TO BE VERY AMUSED BY THESE PICTURES OF YOU AND *FRANK THE GARDENER*.

IT COULDN'T BE ANY WORSE THAN *THIS.*

YOU THINK? IMAGINE YOUR LIFE *RUINED.* YOUR REPUTATION IN *TATTERS...*

I DON'T CARE.

WHAT ABOUT YOUR *FAMILY?* DON'T YOU THINK *THEY'D* BE ASHAMED?

THEY'D BE MORE ASHAMED IF I HELPED A MAN LIKE *YOU.*

THEY RAISED ME TO *STAND UP* TO BULLIES AND THAT'S EXACTLY WHAT I'M DOING NOW. I'M NOT AFRAID OF *ALIENS, ROBOTS, SUPER-VILLAINS* OR *MONSTERS...*

...WHY SHOULD I BE SCARED OF A LITTLE MAN WITH SOME *DIRTY PICTURES?*

HE DROPPED THE ENTIRE THING.

WHAT?

SERIOUSLY, I GOT A TELEGRAM FROM HIS PRIVATE OFFICE SAYING HE WASN'T GOING TO PURSUE IT ANYMORE AND NO FURTHER ACTION WOULD BE TAKEN.

HE EVEN SENT THE NEGATIVES AS A GESTURE OF GOODWILL. I DON'T KNOW WHETHER TO LAUGH OR CRY.

HAVE YOU ANY IDEA *WHY?*

I DON'T KNOW. MAYBE HE WASN'T USED TO SOMEONE STANDING UP TO HIM. MAYBE HE DECIDED IT WASN'T A GOOD IDEA TO PICK A FIGHT WITH SOMEONE WHO *SAVES THE WORLD* THREE TIMES A WEEK.

RICHARD, THIS IS *AMAZING.*

ACTUALLY, IT'S STILL ONLY *HALF* THE PROBLEM SOLVED...

GOOD.

NOW IF YOU'D ALL LIKE TO WATCH THE SCREEN I WANT TO SHOW YOU THIS *INTERSTELLAR ABNORMALITY* I'VE FOUND IN THE EPSILON ERIDANI SYSTEM...

TOLD YOU.

I CAN'T BELIEVE I WAS THE ONLY ONE WHO HAD A PROBLEM WITH A *HOMO* ON THE TEAM.

SHUT UP, WALTER.

WHY DO YOU THINK HE *REALLY* CHANGED HIS MIND?

I LIKE TO IMAGINE BLUE-BOLT JUST APPEALED TO MISTER HOOVER'S *BETTER NATURE*...

DON'T WORRY. WE ALREADY CAUGHT HIM. IT'S CLEANING UP HIS *MARIONETTES* THAT'S GOING TO TAKE ALL NIGHT.

CAN I GET YOU A COFFEE BEFORE YOU GET STARTED?

I'LL TAKE A COFFEE.

MY NAME'S APRIL KELLY.

THE FLARE.

DO YOU REALLY THINK I HAVE WHAT IT TAKES?

DEFINITELY.

THE FLARE & MIRACLE-GIRL BUST CRIME SYNDICATE

IS THIS SOME KIND OF JOKE?

WHAT?

SHE'S A 19-YEAR-OLD GIRL WITH NO SUPER POWERS AND YOU'RE ASKING IF SHE CAN JOIN *THE UNION?*

YOU'RE MAKING A *FOOL* OF YOURSELF, FITZ. WE'RE NOT GOING TO CONDONE THIS RIDICULOUS BEHAVIOR.

NOW HOLD ON A SECOND, GRACE...

NO, YOU HOLD ON. YOU'VE TAKEN THIS GIRL FROM THE MIDDLE OF NOWHERE AND SET HER UP WITH A JOB AND AN APARTMENT.

YOU'RE TAKING ADVANTAGE OF A STARSTRUCK TEENAGER AND YOU NEED TO GET A *GRIP.*

SHE'S *IN LOVE* WITH ME.

NO, YOUR *WIFE* IS IN LOVE WITH YOU.

WE'VE ALL KNOWN JOYCE SINCE WE WERE BACK IN COLLEGE AND WE'RE NOT GOING TO LET YOU *HUMILIATE* HER LIKE THIS.

SO RICHIE'S ALLOWED TO HAVE *BOYFRIENDS*, BUT I CAN'T DATE A *GIRL?*

THANKS A LOT.

PRETTY MUCH.

END THIS NOW OR YOU'RE OFF THE TEAM.

SAMMY'S BAR:

SO WHAT DID YOU DO?

WHAT DO YOU *THINK* I DID? I BROKE UP WITH HER LIKE A GOOD LITTLE *SUPERHERO.*

DEEP DOWN, I KNEW IT WAS FOR THE BEST. MY OLD MAN WALKED OUT WHEN I WAS NINE YEARS OLD AND ALL THAT IT TAUGHT ME WAS NOTHING EVER *LASTS.*

"WHEN THINGS GET TOUGH YOU THROW IN THE TOWEL...

April

"...THAT NOBODY IN LIFE EVER KEEPS THEIR *PROMISES*..."

...I DIDN'T WANT MY KIDS LEARNING THAT FROM *ME*.

SO YOU'RE *HAPPY* BEING BACK IN YOUR OLD LIFE AGAIN?

ARE YOU KIDDING? I'M MISERABLE AS SIN. BUT THAT'S THE THING WHEN YOU BECOME A PARENT. THE KIDS COME *FIRST*.

AND THAT'S THE LESSON YOU'RE TEACHING YOUR CHILDREN? TO STAY IN SOMETHING EVEN WHEN THEY'RE *MISERABLE*?

IF *I'D* MET SOMEONE I THOUGHT I LOVED I'M NOT SURE I'D HAVE *GIVEN UP* SO EASILY.

WHAT IF THIS WAS YOUR *BIG SHOT,* MAC? WHAT IF THIS NEVER HAPPENS AGAIN?

400 MILES AWAY:

CHAPTER 4

GOD, I'D LOVE TO BE IN A SUPER-TEAM. I STILL CAN'T BELIEVE THEY DIDN'T LET ME JOIN *THE UNION.*

WELL, YOU'RE MORE THAN WELCOME HERE. YOU DON'T NEED TO HAVE SUPER-POWERS TO JOIN US. WE'RE PRETTY RELAXED ABOUT STUFF LIKE THAT.

YOU'RE *TOO OLD* TO JOIN THE TEEN SCENE. YOU'LL BE *TWENTY* IN A MONTH.

SO SHE'S STILL TECHNICALLY NINETEEN.

DON'T BE RIDICULOUS. WHY WOULD SHE JOIN SOMETHING SHE HAS TO *LEAVE* IN FOUR WEEKS?

TAKE IT EASY, APRIL. THEY'LL LET YOU IN THE UNION NOW THAT WE'RE *ENGAGED.*

SO HOW ARE THE KIDS?

THE LITTLE ONES ARE CONFUSED. PETER'S JUST ANGRY.

I DON'T THINK FITZ REALIZES WHAT A FOOL HE'S MAKING OF HIMSELF. SHE'S *HALF HIS AGE*, GRACE.

AREN'T THEY *ALWAYS?*

I JUST WISH HE'D STOP RUBBING OUR FACES IN IT WITH ALL THE *MAGAZINE COVERS* AND *HOLLYWOOD PARTIES.*

THAT'S WHAT'S GOING TO BE THE HARDEST THING TO GET OVER WHEN HE COMES BACK HOME. THIS CONSTANT HUMILIATION.

WHAT MAKES YOU THINK HE'S *COMING HOME*, JOYCE?

I'VE KNOWN HIM SINCE WE WERE TWENTY-ONE YEARS OLD. I KNOW FITZ BETTER THAN HE KNOWS *HIMSELF.*

I HEAR YOUR *POWERS* ARE STARTING TO DEVELOP.

STRENGTH AND SPEED, BUT NOTHING *UNIQUE* YET, UNCLE SHELDON.

YOU'RE A LUCKY BOY. RICKY BODEN'S ALMOST OUT OF HIGH SCHOOL AND HASN'T HAD A THING YET. JUST BECAUSE YOUR *OLD MAN'S* GOT POWERS DOESN'T MEAN *ANYTHING*.

WHAT'S YOUR PLAN WHEN THEY *DO* SHOW UP? ARE YOU GOING TO JOIN THE *TEEN SCENE?*

NOPE...

I'M GOING TO KILL MY DAD.

IS HE GOING TO BE OKAY, RICHARD?

I DON'T THINK SO.

THE NEUROLOGIST SAID HE'S DAMAGED EVERYTHING FROM THE NECK DOWN.

THE BREAKS LITERALLY COULDN'T HAVE HAPPENED IN WORSE PLACES. EVERY MOTOR FUNCTION IS COMPLETELY IMPAIRED.

OH NO.

WHY DOES THIS KEEP HAPPENING? WHY ARE WE ALWAYS STANDING HERE PRAYING FOR A PAL IN *ICU*?

IT'S NOT ALL BALLOONS AND PARADES, GEORGE. THIS IS THE FLIP-SIDE OF THE JOB AND WE KNOW THE RISKS GOING IN.

I'M ONLY *NINETEEN*, FOR CHRIST'S SAKE.

DON'T WORRY, SWEETHEART. I KNOW.

HAVE YOU GOT SOMEWHERE TO STAY TONIGHT?

YEAH...

JEFF'S PUTTING ME UP AT *TEEN SCENE*.

CHAPTER 5

CUTHBERT THE BUTLER IS A BIG PART OF THE PROBLEM. IT DOESN'T MATTER WHAT GEORGE GETS UP TO, CUTHBERT'S ALWAYS THERE TO PICK UP THE *PIECES*.

YOUR EGGS, MASTER GEORGE, THE YOLKS HARDENED IN VARYING DEGREES FROM NUMBER ONE TO NINETY-NINE.

I THINK I'LL GO FOR A *SEVENTY-TWO* THIS MORNING, CUTHBERT.

BUSY DAY AHEAD, SIR?

JUST MAKING PLANS FOR LIFE AFTER DEATH.

COME AND SEE.

WHO WOULD HAVE THOUGHT *GEORGE HUTCHENCE* COULD BE SO SAPPY?

HE'S LIKE A DIFFERENT PERSON.

WELL, WHAT DID SHE SAY?

Chapter 6

"HOW DO YOU THINK HE'LL TAKE IT?"

GEORGE? REALLY BADLY.

IT'S NOT THE FACT I'M SEEING SOMEONE ELSE. IT'S THE FACT THAT YOU'RE ANOTHER *SUPERHERO*, WALTER.

HOW DID YOU MANAGE TO GET PARIS SO *PERFECT?* IT'S LIKE WE'RE WALKING AROUND IN THE *MOVIE.*

WELL, I HAVEN'T ACTUALLY SEEN IT YET, BUT ALL THESE LITTLE *MOMENTS* FROM *BREATHLESS* WERE LODGED QUITE DEEP IN YOUR SUBCONSCIOUS MIND.

LET'S *READ* SOMETHING TOGETHER. COULD WE EAVESDROP ON J.D. SALINGER'S THOUGHTS? OR MAYBE HARPER LEE'S NEXT THING?

DON'T YOU WANT TO DO SOMETHING IN REAL LIFE FOR A CHANGE?

I'M TIRED OF HIDING. IT'S LIKE WE'RE *ASHAMED.*

DON'T. YOU *KNOW* WHY WE'RE DOING THIS.

YOU'RE TAKING *WALTER'S* SIDE? AFTER ALL THESE *YEARS?*

SHE'S MET SOMEONE ELSE, GEORGE. JUST *ACCEPT* IT.

YOU CAN *ALL* GO TO HELL.

SEEMS A LITTLE PARANOID WHEN THERE ARE BARELY FIFTY *ACTIVE* OUT THERE.

BUT THEY *BREED,* DEAR BROTHER. A WISE MAN ALWAYS THINKS AHEAD.

DID YOU LIKE MY LITTLE THANK YOU TO GEORGE, BY THE WAY? HE AND I MIGHT HAVE HAD OUR QUARRELS, BUT HE'S STILL THE SUPERMAX'S *ORIGINAL DESIGNER.*

CAN I ASK YOU SOMETHING, WALTER?

FEEL FREE.

THAT FEELING GEORGE HAD THAT YOU USED YOUR PSYCHIC POWERS TO BREAK UP HIM AND SUNNY...

...IT ISN'T *TRUE,* IS IT?

WEECOOWEEOOOWEEOOOWEEOOO

KENTUCKY:

WEEOOOWEEOOOWEEOOOWEEOOO

OH MY! WHAT'S GOING ON OUT THERE?

ARMED ROBBERY, MOST LIKELY.

WEEOOOWEEOOOWEEOOOWEEOOO

GOODNESS!

THESE THINGS *HAPPEN.*

THANKS FOR THE COFFEE, MA'AM. KEEP THE CHANGE.

TO BE CONTINUED

MARK MILLAR

Mark Millar is the *New York Times* bestselling author of *Kick-Ass*, *Wanted*, and *Kingsman: The Secret Service*, all of which have been adapted into Hollywood franchises.

His DC Comics work includes the seminal *Superman: Red Son*. At Marvel Comics he created *The Ultimates*, which was selected by *Time* magazine as the comic book of the decade, and was described by screenwriter Zak Penn as his major inspiration for *The Avengers* movie. Millar also created *Wolverine: Old Man Logan* and *Civil War*, Marvel's two biggest-selling graphic novels ever. *Civil War* was the basis of the *Captain America: Civil War* movie, and *Old Man Logan* was the inspiration for Fox's *Logan* movie in 2017.

Mark has been an executive producer on all his movies, and for four years worked as a creative consultant to Fox Studios on their Marvel slate of movies. In 2017, Netflix bought Millarworld in the company's first ever acquisition, and employed Mark as President of a new division to create comics, TV shows, and movies. His much-anticipated autobiography, *In His Eyes Rest The Stories*, will be published next year.

WILFREDO TORRES

Wilfredo Torres is a self-taught American comic book artist and illustrator. He has been working as a professional freelancer since 2007. Before his work with Mark Millar on *Jupiter's Circle,* Wilfredo was best known for his work on *The Shadow: Year One* (Dynamite Entertainment), *Batman '66* (DC Comics), *Lobster Johnson: Prayer of Neferu* (Dark Horse Comics), and *Quantum & Woody* (Valiant Entertainment). Wilfredo redesigned and provided covers for *The Shield* (Archie Comics/Dark Circle).

Wilfredo is a process junkie who enjoys sleeping, pictures of puppies, home improvement shows, beer, long walks, and drawing people who wear their underwear over their clothes.

DAVIDE GIANFELICE

Davide Gianfelice was born in Milan, Italy in 1977. Before his collaboration on *Jupiter's Circle*, he worked for Vertigo on the acclaimed first run of *Northlanders* and *Greek Street.* His work for Marvel comics can be seen in *Daredevil: Reborn, Wolverine: Weapon X*, and *Six Guns.*

With Dark Horse he collaborated on a run of *Conan the Barbarian,* and with Skybound he provided art for *Ghosted.* In his spare time he enjoys cooking Italian food and has a passion for photography.

FRANCESCO MORTARINO

Francesco Mortarino was born in 1978 in Milan, Italy. After graduating from the Comics School of Milano, he started working for Italian publishers like Edizioni BD in 2008.

In 2014 he started to work with Sergio Bonelli Editore on the *Nathan Never* comic book.

In 2015 he was very proud to collaborate with Davide Gianfelice on the art for *Jupiter's Circle.*

He lives in Milan with his wife and their two terrific children.

IVE SVORCINA

Ive was born in 1986 on a small island in the Adriatic Sea, Croatia. Being self-taught, he somehow managed to start his professional career in 2006, and since then he has worked for such publishers as Marvel, Delcourt, Image Comics, and smaller publishers in Croatia.

Notable achievements include getting kicked out of the computer science college and getting nominated for an Eisner award for his work on *Thor*.

Currently he resides in Zagreb, and is thinking about moving somewhere warmer and sunnier.

PETER DOHERTY

Peter's earliest work in comics was during 1990, providing painted artwork for the John Wagner-written *Young Death: The Boyhood of a Superfiend*, published in the first year of the *Judge Dredd Megazine*.
For the next few years he painted art for a number of Judge Dredd stories.

Over the intervening years he's worked for most of the major comics publishers, and also branched out into illustration, TV, and movie work.

Over the last decade he's worked on projects both as the sole artist and as a coloring/lettering/design collaborator with other artists, including Geof Darrow on his *Shaolin Cowboy* project, and most recently Frank Quitely and Duncan Fegredo, on the Millarworld projects *Jupiter's Legacy* and *MPH,* respectively.

Peter lives locally, in the Yorkshire countryside.

NICOLE BOOSE

Nicole Boose began her comics career as an assistant editor for Harris Comics' *Vampirella,* before joining the editorial staff at Marvel Comics. There, she edited titles including *Cable & Deadpool, Invincible Iron Man,* and Stephen King's *Dark Tower* adaptations, and oversaw Marvel's line of custom comic publications.

Since 2008, Nicole has worked as a freelance editor and consultant in the comics industry, with editorial credits that include the Millarworld titles *Superior, Super Crooks, Jupiter's Legacy, MPH, Starlight,* and *Chrononauts.* Nicole is also Communications Manager for Comics Experience, an online school and community for comic creators.

Born in Philadelphia and a long-time New Yorker, she now lives near Cleveland, Ohio with her family.

FIND OUT WHAT HAPPENS NEXT

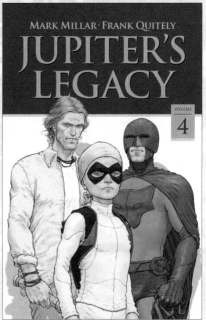

NETFLIX